PUCCINI
AND THE PROWLERS

NIGHTWOOD EDITIONS
P.O. Box 2079
Sechelt, BC Canada V0N 3A0

Design by Roger Handling

Canadian Cataloguing in Publication Data

Wiseman, Adele, 1928–1992.
  Puccini and the prowlers

  ISBN 0-88971-154-2

  I. LaFave, Kim.   II. Title.
PS8545.I85P8 1992   jC813'.54   C92-091716-X
PZ7.W57Pu 1992

PUCCINI
AND THE PROWLERS

STORY BY
ADELE WISEMAN
ILLUSTRATIONS BY
KIM LA FAVE

NIGHTWOOD EDITIONS

Puccini was a hard barking pup. That was because he knew his job. Ever since the time he had heard his boy, Cameron, tell his friend Ziggy, "My poochy protects our house from prowlers," he had known the kind of dog he was, and it made him very proud. He made up his mind that he would go on protecting the house from prowlers, as hard as he could.

Only one thing puzzled him. He didn't quite know what a prowler was. At first he thought it must be a cat, so he made a great war on any cats who dared to come near the lawn. But there were very few cats around, so Puccini thought perhaps a prowler was a bird. After that no bird would dare to settle on their lawn. Puccini barked them right back up the trees where they belonged.

Next he began to suspect that a prowler was a postman. But the postman was much bigger than the birds and cats, and Pucci was only a little pup after all, so whenever the postman came into the yard Puccini ran a little distance away before he even dared turn around to ask him if he was a prowler. But he asked him. He wasn't going to let a prowler get away with anything.

"Are you a prowler?" he yapped, in his squeaky pup's voice. "Are you a prowler? If you're a prowler I'll chase you away!" he barked frantically. "I will! I will I will I will!!!"

But the postman couldn't understand
Puccini's questions and he merely grumbled
about how much he hated yapping pups.
    "Whadja say? Whadja say?" shouted
Puccini, running after him at a safe distance
as he went to the gate. But the postman did
not reply. "He sure behaved suspiciously,"
growled Puccini, when the postman had
gone. "But I got rid of him."

The milkman was a prowler next, and
after him came the butcher prowler. A little
later in the day, after two sparrow prowlers
had been warned off, Puccini showed a
mother cat he meant business by making her
walk her three kittens along the fence rail.
Then the breadman prowler arrived, followed
by the garbageman prowler. In fact Puccini
got hardly a moment's rest all day.

When Cameron came home from school they played a few wild games together. Puccini liked especially the game in which Cameron pretended to be a prowler and Puccini barked at him hard.

By the time bedtime came around Puccini
was all tuckered out. He simply flopped down
in his box and fell asleep, though even in his
sleep he would sometimes growl and snap his
teeth, because he was dreaming of prowlers.

Once, when he awoke in the middle of the night and looked out the window, Puccini saw the moon move slowly across the sky close by. "Aha! Another prowler! He won't get away with this!" And Puccini set up such a howling that he woke up the whole house and half the neighbourhood. And he wouldn't stop, either, until Father came down and gave him a good talking to. Even then he grumbled and complained as he curled up again in his box. "People don't appreciate you. They don't know what's good for them."

"I said be quiet, Pucci!" came Father's stern voice from the doorway, and Puccini had to stop complaining and nurse his hurt feelings in silence, with every now and then an angry glance at the moon. "Some people," he told himself, "think more of their prowlers than they do of their pups." He even thought of running away that night, but in the morning, when Cameron hugged him, he decided maybe he'd give them another chance.

Though Puccini was doing his best to protect them the neighbours didn't appreciate all the noise he was making. "There goes that yappy pup again," they would say. "You'd think a pup would be able to think of something better to do than bark all day. And he's really such a nice little dog. All you have to do is pet him and he stops barking."

This was perfectly true. Puccini didn't think that anyone who was nice to him could really be a prowler, and if the postman and the milkman and the garbageman and the baker had taken a little trouble to make friends they might not have got such a noisy reception every day.

Of course he would probably have gone on barking at the cats and the birds, just to keep in practice, but Puccini would much rather have been friends with all the people who came to the house. If only they would stop behaving like prowlers and make friends with a pup!

In fact, once a stranger did take the trouble to make friends with Puccini. He gave him a little bite to eat, rubbed him behind the ears, called him nice names in a soft voice, and Pucci didn't bark at him at all. For Puccini was a dog of principle. He barked only at prowlers, not at nice people.

That was the man who walked away with
all the laundry off the line in broad daylight,
early one Monday morning.

Puccini got a lot of attention from the family that day.

"What were you doing, Pucci?" asked Mother in a soft, puzzled voice, shaking her head. "Where were you when it happened? How come you didn't bark?"

"Dumb dog," groaned Father, "dumb dog!"

Puccini was puzzled.

Was Father as angry as he seemed, or was this just another game? Just to be safe, Puccini hung his head down and put his tail between his legs the way he did when he was really frightened and begging to make up.

He even managed a small whimper.

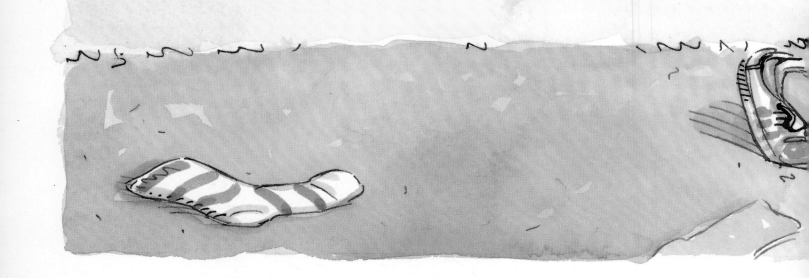

"Don't cry, Pucci," said Cameron. "You can't help it if you're a dumb dog. I love you anyway."

Puccini waited till Cameron had bent right down close to him and quick as a flash he nipped at his nose, and got Cameron's face all wet.

"Hey!" yelled Cameron, and jumped him. Pretty soon dog and boy were rolling about the floor, yelling and yapping.

"Never mind," said Mother, "even if he isn't a watchdog, he's a sweet little pup."

"And he makes a noise like a watchdog," sighed Father, "which is enough to fool all honest people anyway."

And Puccini went on protecting his
people against prowlers, even though they
didn't know it.